P9-CFE-360

Dear Komodo Dragon

by Nancy Kelly Allen
illustrated by
Laurie Allen Klein

Over on Komodo Island
living, breathing dragons,
giant, man-eating dragons,
sharp-clawed and fierce,
stomp through woods
and lurk in the grass,
ready to attack.

These are Komodo dragons,
real dragons,
and one is my pen pal.

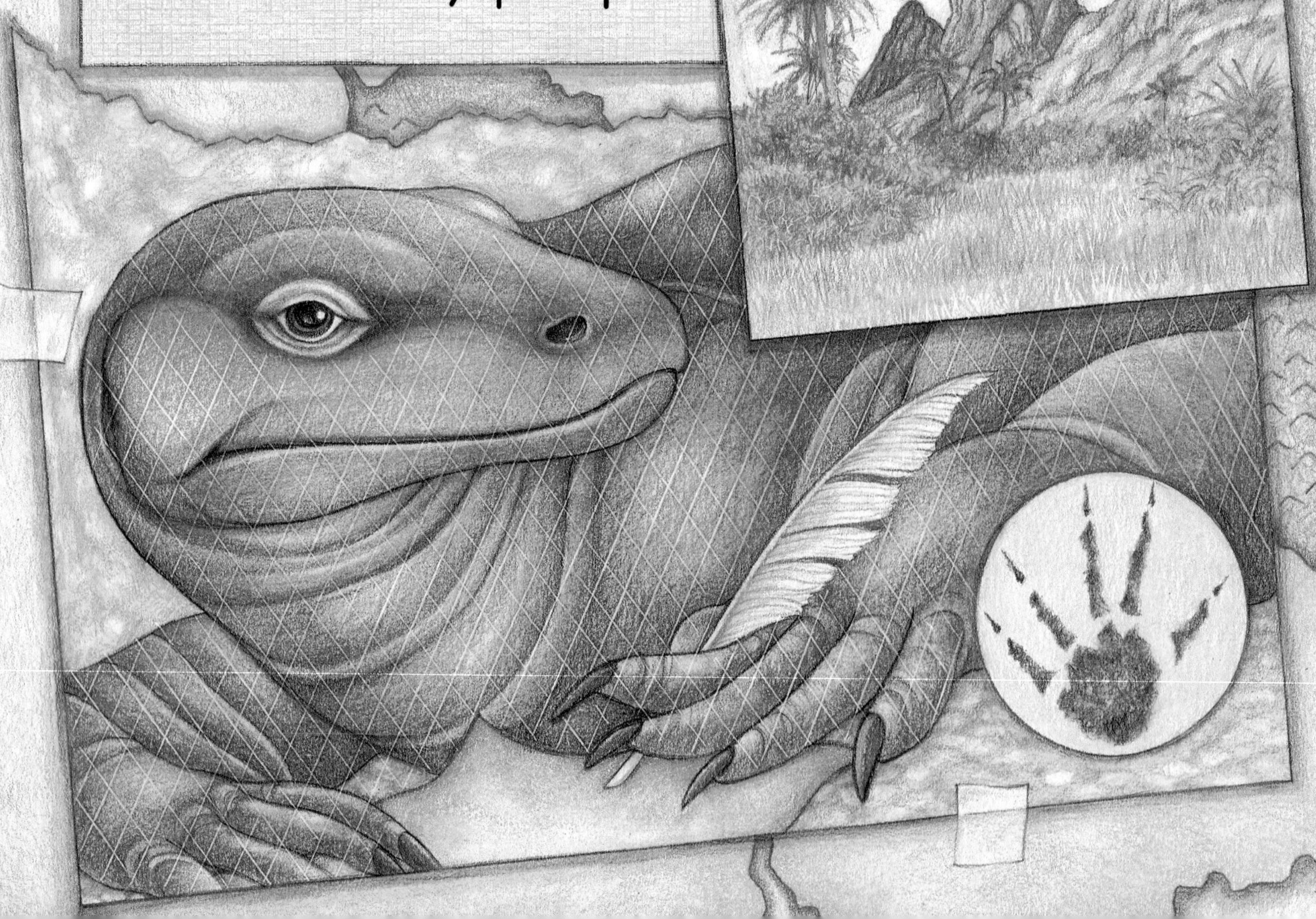

HERE
BE
DRAGONS
KOMODO
RINCA
FLORES

Dear Komodo Dragon,

I've never seen a real dragon, but I've always wanted to. Tell me something about you.

Sincerely,

Leslie

P.S. I'm going to be dragon hunter when I grow up.

ORA

ME (LESLIE)

Lindworm
Wyvern
Asian Lung
European Dragon

Dear Dragon Hunter Leslie,

I'm not bragging when I say Komodo dragons are the biggest and heaviest lizards. My daddy is ten feet long. About half of my body is my tail and that's a handy thing to have. It propels me through water, and I can use it as a weapon in a fight.

My spiffy good looks come from my third eye in the top of my head. It helps me sense when the light changes.

See ya (but not with my 3rd eye),

Komo

Dear Komo,

Do you have any brothers and sisters? If not, you can have mine. Hee! Hee!

More than I need,

Les

Dear More Les,

I come from a big nest of eggs, twenty. After hatching, I've been living in a tree to stay safe from predators, such as wild boars and Komodo dragons. That's right, little Komodo dragons must beware of big ones. We are tasty snacks.

At almost four years old and four feet long, I'm getting too big to climb a tree. I moved to the ground last night. The night air was cold so I dug a burrow in the dirt to stay warm. I'm cold-blooded, so my body is the same temperature as the air.

Life is good,
Komo

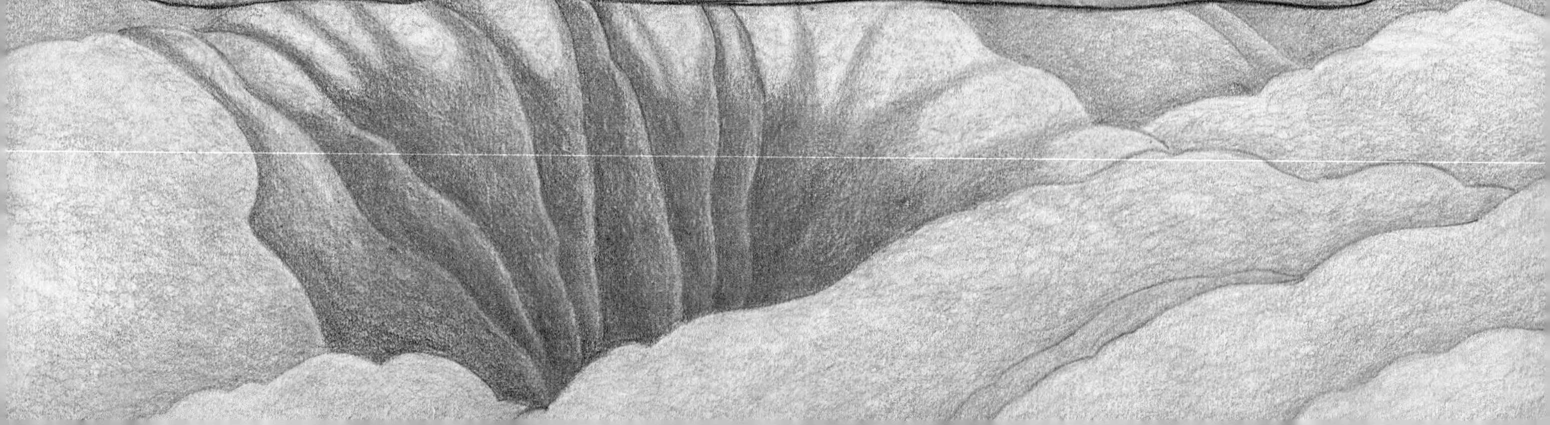

Dear Komo,

Wow, a treehouse!

Is catching prey hard work? Do you eat people?

A picky eater,

Les

Dear Picky Les,

The tall grass camouflages me as I prowl. Flicking my tongue in and out, I smell for prey. Sometimes minutes, sometimes hours, I wait. When a goat wanders by, I attack. Patient fellow, that's me.

I'm a carnivore so I eat anything that's meat. My favorite meal is carrion, dead animals. You may know it as "roadkill." I know it as DEE-licious! Besides, if I eat old, sick, or injured animals, they don't spread diseases. I should be given some kind of health award. Maybe I'm a hero.

Komodos don't bother people, usually. Carry a big stick. We'll back away.

Not picky,

Komo

Dear Komo,

Does eating a big meal give you a bellyache? That's what happens to me when I pig out on pizza.

Feeling stuffed,

Les

Dear Stuffed Les,

I don't remember ever having a belly ache, but after a big meal, my belly drags on the ground. By then I need a drink so I mosey over to a water hole. What do you like to do after a big meal? Take a nap, right? Me, too. A nap in a sunny spot helps my food digest. I'm all for good health.

The parts I can't digest—hair, claws, bones, and feathers—I cough up. Heave ho! I call that my power spew. A.K.A. gastric pellet.

A belly-draggin' dragon,

Komo

Dear Draggin' Dragon,

Since you are a dragon, please answer my question. Do Komodo dragons spit fire?

Curious,

Les

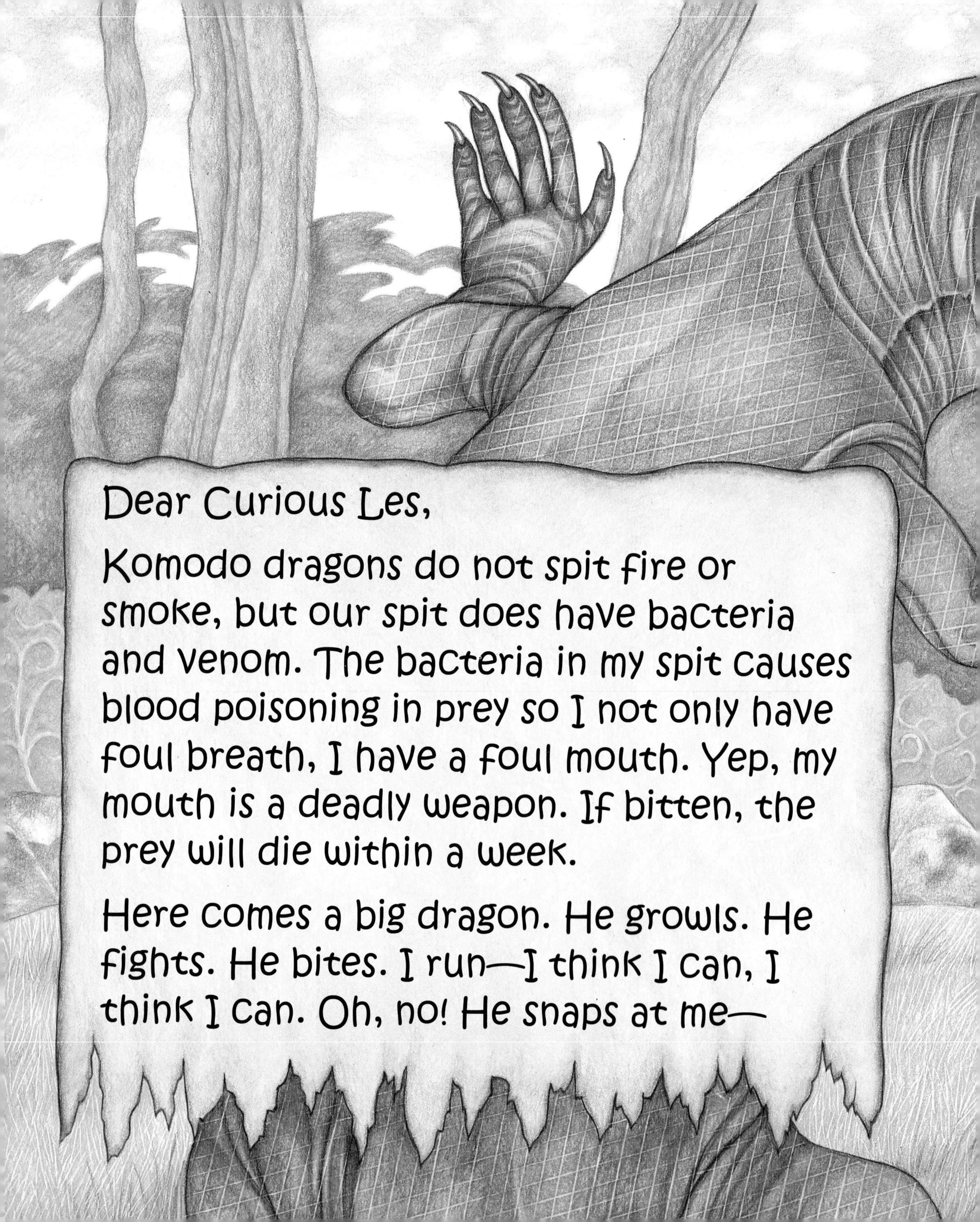

Dear Curious Les,

Komodo dragons do not spit fire or smoke, but our spit does have bacteria and venom. The bacteria in my spit causes blood poisoning in prey so I not only have foul breath, I have a foul mouth. Yep, my mouth is a deadly weapon. If bitten, the prey will die within a week.

Here comes a big dragon. He growls. He fights. He bites. I run—I think I can, I think I can. Oh, no! He snaps at me—

Komodo Friends

Dear Komo,

I have been so worried about you. Did you escape? I know I said I wanted to be a Komodo dragon hunter when I grow up, but that was before I got to know you. What can I do to help you and other Komodo dragons?

A friend,
Les

Dear Friend Les,

I escaped, but the big Komodo dragon bit me and chased me away from dinner. Biting me is no big deal. I'm immune to the dragon's venom. How do you like my snazzy new bandages? Get this—for the next few weeks, I'll be known as "Wrap-tile."

Komodos don't have many predators, except humans. Yep, some people are real dragon hunters who break the law and poach Komodos. Natural disasters—earthquakes and erupting volcanoes—spell danger, too.

You are a good sport to help keep us alive. There are only about 3,000 of us in the world so spread the word that we should be seen and not killed.

Your friend,

Wrap-tile

For Creative Minds

This section may be photocopied or printed from our website by the owner of this book for educational, non-commercial use. Cross-curricular teaching activities for use at home or in the classroom, interactive quizzes, and more are available online.

Visit www.ArbordalePublishing.com to explore additional resources.

Dragons by the Numbers

1
number of months a Komodo dragon can go without food
I'm so stuffed, I couldn't eat for a month!

300
pounds (136 kg) a full-grown Komodo dragon weighs with a full belly
I'm big, I'm bad, and I'm on the hunt.

5
number of islands where Komodo dragons live in the wild
It's a little snug, but it's home.

1980
year Komodo National Park was established
Finally! Those humans were eating me out of house and home.

13
baby Komodo dragons hatched at the National Zoo in 1992
Well, this isn't my island . . .

3,000
estimated number of Komodo dragons left in the world
We'd better get hatching!

30
years in a Komodo dragon's lifespan
I'll be an old dragon by the time you finish college!

95
degrees Fahrenheit (35 °C) in Komodo dragons' natural habitat
Ahh, nice and warm.

Conservation

Komodo dragons live in Indonesia, a country in Southeast Asia. These giant reptiles have been around for millions of years. They are the largest living lizards in the world!

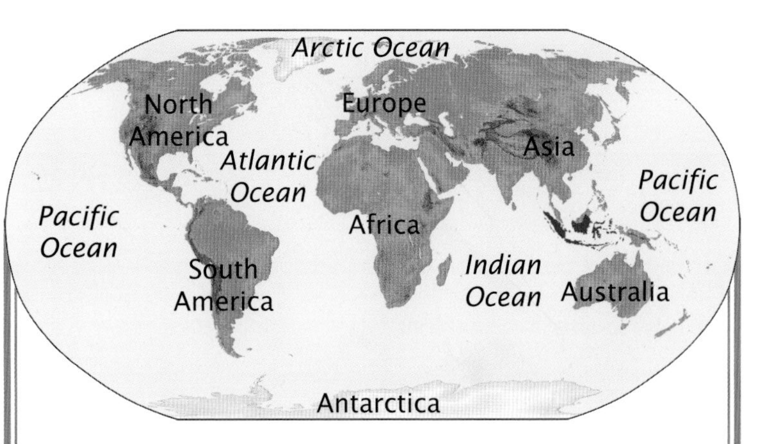

This world map shows Indonesia in red. If you traveled from Africa to Indonesia, what ocean would you cross? If you traveled from North America to Indonesia, what ocean would you cross?

Remember that the Earth is shaped like a ball (globe). A map is a flattened image of that globe.

There are many threats to Komodo dragons. Humans and Komodo dragons both like to eat deer and pigs. If people overhunt the prey on an island, there is not enough food left for Komodo dragons. Natural disasters, like earthquakes and volcanoes, can destroy their habitat. A large human population shares the island of Flores with Komodo dragons. This can lead to problems.

Komodo dragons need help so that they don't die out. The Indonesian government protects them. On the islands of Komodo, Rinca, Gila Montag, and Gili Dasami, the Komodo dragons live in the wild. Humans are banned from hunting on these islands. Game wardens work in the park to stop hunters from poaching the lizards and their prey.

Scientists and conservationists in Indonesia and around the world can help Komodo dragons. Many local people work to protect their special lizards. There are Komodo dragons in more than 30 zoos. These zoos teach the public about Komodo dragons.

You can help protect Komodo dragons too! The United States is the world's largest market for animal products. You should not buy products made from Komodo dragons or their prey.

Physical and Behavioral Adaptations

An adaptation helps animals live in their habitat. It helps them get food and water, protect themselves from predators, survive weather, and even make their homes.

Adaptations can be physical or behavioral. **Physical adaptations** affect animals' bodies. **Behavioral adaptations** affect the way an animal acts. Komodo dragons have both physical and behavioral adaptations that help them live in their habitat.

Sort the following traits into physical or behavioral adaptations.

A. Komodo dragons have a third eye on top of their heads. They can sense light and dark with this eye.

B. Razor-sharp teeth and strong jaws and neck muscles help the dragons hunt and feed. If they lose any teeth, they can regrow them.

C. Food can be scarce so they eat quickly before another Komodo dragon arrives and fights them for the food.

D. They have bacteria and venom in their mouths. Once bitten, the prey escapes but soon dies. The dragon follows and feasts.

E. They are aggressive and will attack animals, even other Komodo dragons. This behavior protects their territory and food supply.

F. Komodo dragons feed on any animal they can catch. They often attack animals that are larger than themselves, such as water buffalo.

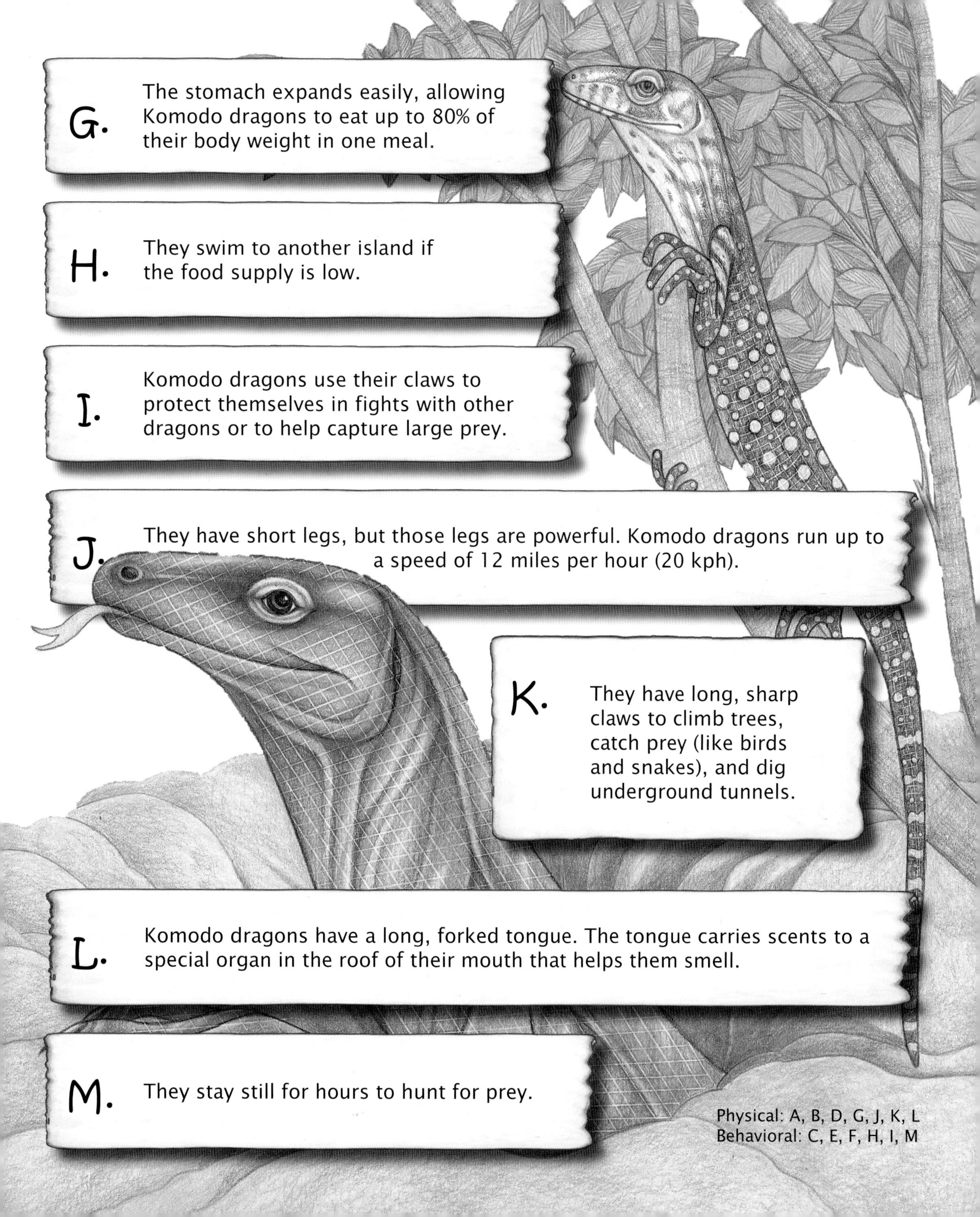

G. The stomach expands easily, allowing Komodo dragons to eat up to 80% of their body weight in one meal.

H. They swim to another island if the food supply is low.

I. Komodo dragons use their claws to protect themselves in fights with other dragons or to help capture large prey.

J. They have short legs, but those legs are powerful. Komodo dragons run up to a speed of 12 miles per hour (20 kph).

K. They have long, sharp claws to climb trees, catch prey (like birds and snakes), and dig underground tunnels.

L. Komodo dragons have a long, forked tongue. The tongue carries scents to a special organ in the roof of their mouth that helps them smell.

M. They stay still for hours to hunt for prey.

Physical: A, B, D, G, J, K, L
Behavioral: C, E, F, H, I, M

For Ava and Harper—NKA

To BK and JK, always my Muse and Inspiration—LAK

Thanks to Christine Lewis and Kate Davis, Zoo Educators at the Birmingham Zoo, and to Alison F. Manka, School and Aquarium Programs Manager at the Greensboro Science Center, for verifying the accuracy of the information in this book.

Library of Congress Cataloging-in-Publication Data

Names: Allen, Nancy Kelly, 1949- author. | Klein, Laurie Allen, illustrator.
Title: Dear Komodo Dragon / by Nancy Kelly Allen ; illustrated by Laurie Allen Klein.
Description: Mount Pleasant, SC : Arbordale Publishing, [2018] | Includes bibliographical references. | Summary: Leslie, a young girl who plans to be a dragon hunter one day, becomes pen pals with Komo, a Komodo dragon who tells her all about himself and dangers to his species. Includes a section with additional facts.
Identifiers: LCCN 2017040943| ISBN 9781607184492 (English hardcover) | ISBN 9781607184607 (English pbk.) | ISBN 9781607184652 (Spanish pbk.) | ISBN 9781607184829 (English Downloadable eBook) | ISBN 9781607184997 (English Interactive Dual-Language eBook) | ISBN 9781607184874 (Spanish Downloadable eBook) | ISBN 9781607185185 (Spanish interactive dual-language ebook)
Subjects: LCSH: Komodo dragon--Juvenile fiction. | Komodo dragon--Fiction. | CYAC: Letters.
Classification: LCC PZ10.3.A4277 De 2018 | DDC [E]--dc23 LC record available at https://lccn.loc.gov/2017040943

Translated into Spanish: ***Querido Dragón Komodo***

Lexile® Level: 630L

key phrases: conservation, environmental education, dragons, komodo dragons

Bibliography:
Attenborough, David. *Life in Cold Blood.* Princeton, NJ: Princeton UP, 2008. Print.
Murphy, James B. *Komodo Dragons: Biology and Conservation.* Washington, D.C.: Smithsonian Institution, 2002. Print.

Manufactured in China, December 2017
This product conforms to CPSIA 2008
First Printing

Arbordale Publishing
Mt. Pleasant, SC 29464
www.ArbordalePublishing.com